A WRITER'S COVE:
The Night Owls Collective

Vol. 1

Tracie E. Gumola
Robin E. Thorpe
Valerie D Wade
Toni M. Whitney

Compiled by
Sarah E. Whitney

About The Authors

Marie Louise Batchelor, a vibrant and loving individual, was born in Detroit to parents who had immigrated from Trinidad, BWI. She was a dedicated mother to five children and a cherished grandmother to sixteen. From a young age, she showed a passion for playing the piano and found joy in activities such as coloring, writing, and listening to jazz music. Known for her boundless energy and zest for life, she left a lasting impact on everyone she met.

Tracie E. Gumola has been writing since elementary school. Her love of poetry was inspired to bloom by the works of early favorites, Langston Hughes, and Shel Silverstein. Finding a creative, emotional, and intellectual outlet in the magic of pen to paper, she embraced this journey to find a lifelong haven and boundless sounding board.

Author **Robin E. Thorpe** began writing at the age of twelve by drafting personal poems for family and friends. Many years later she was awarded a diploma from The Longridge Writers Group upon completion of their course Writing for Publication. For several years, she created stories and skits for Children's ministry, family members, teachers, and their students. As she matured, she wrote magazine articles for Senior citizens adding a bit of wisdom and humor to the aging process. She is a mother of five and grandmother who now resides as an empty nester with her husband in Detroit, MI and is currently working on the completion of her first novel entitled, "*The Other Hand.*"

Valerie D. Wade, author of Ivy Lee's Rue and Leaving Jacksonville, is thrilled to see this family collaboration come to life. She is a lifelong resident of Detroit, Michigan, having grown up in Highland Park,

Michigan. Valerie is an alumna of Wayne State University, and currently works as a Research Administrator. She has published poetry, is a volunteer literacy tutor, loves spending time with her adult children and grandchildren, and plans to pursue her dream of learning to play drums.

Sarah E. Whitney is a clinical social worker from Southfield, Michigan. While she loves her career in mental health therapy, her passions for storytelling and family healing have culminated in this anthology.

Toni M. Whitney is a frustrated writer. She is a mother of six and grandmother of four. She has lived many lives and had many careers including homemaker, bookkeeper, office manager, paraeducator, and now in her retirement, author. Toni's interests are crocheting, reading, and spending time with her grandchildren.

Dedication

We hold this volume of work in a special place in our hearts as we dedicate it to some treasured family members we have lost over the years. We wish to honor their memories by sharing a few details about their lives. Our parents and grandparents, **James William Sherman** and **Marie Louise Batchelor**, were filled with an abundance of love and always prioritized their family above all else. They instilled in us the values of hard work, honesty, and kindness, which have guided us throughout our lives.

Our grandfather and great grandfather, **Rupert Eugene Braithwaite (Papa)**, was a proud man of great wisdom and strength who immigrated from Trinidad, BWI. He taught us the importance of perseverance, strong family values, and his unwavering faith will always inspire us.

Lastly, we remember our siblings/aunt/uncle, **William Emanual Sherman** and **Kris Jeanne Sherman-Burns**, who left us much too soon. We will always remember them for bringing joy and laughter into our lives.

In dedicating this work to their memories, we hope to preserve their legacies and honor their lives. We believe that their spirits will live on through our family and that their examples will continue to guide us for generations to come.

Table of Contents

Chapter 1

Discovery

Pour Open!

Tracie Elaine

Let my heart pour open for future fans
Fans of love and fantastical romance
Spin a rhyme or two in jest
Jest against negative vibes & unrest

Take my hand & I'll show you a new way
Way to seize more sugar in your sour day
Lazy I may be in work, but primed for play
Play that drowns out the sound of the gloomy gray

If we haven't met, won't you please join the band?
Band of free spirits in an uptight land
Can we revive a harmony lost in the quicksand?
Quicksand that has shackled the precious soul of man..........

A Moment of Bliss

By Robin E. Thorpe

In the presence of his glory I sat. Warm breezes engulfed my body as I became mesmerized by the beautiful view.

The golden sand whispered my name calling for the exfoliation of my feet and toes. Perhaps I could have derived some pleasure from the warmth and grainy massage, yet I resisted.

My desire was only for the breeze and the sparkle of sunlit ripples of water; how gentle was their kiss upon the shore.

Occasionally boats drifted by causing a deeper wave, creating mellow splashes of aquatic bliss.

Clouds of fluffy white entranced me, giving the appearance of distant snow-covered mountains floating at a snail's pace in the pastel blue sky.

Brief moments of welcomed freedom seduced our humanity offering the bliss of an unmasked face, wondering if our Canadian neighbors glance our way, as we do them, experiencing the serenity of a distant shore,

In harmony we embrace the full splendor of our gift of this moment,

If only I could fly...

Tracie Elaine

if only I could fly
fly into the window
window of your dreams
dreams of me moonstruck
moonstruck and swimming
swimming ahead of the waves
waves rolling along the grass
grass translated in air
air delighted to the wind
wind inspired would curtsy
curtsy & call on the motherland
motherland awake and sleeping
sleeping upon ginger & cushion
cushion of black hills and islands
islands of echoing tides
tides of my familiar.......

Our Imperfect World

By Robin E. Thorpe

If nothing ever changes and today is all we have, our imperfect little world inside this universe.

If today is all there is, and tomorrow no longer exists and all we have is now, and who we are, is all we will ever be, right here in this moment.

I'm right here with the one whom I want my forever to always be with.
Could any tomorrow be my tomorrow without my imperfect little today?
The love I know, the love I want, the love I need, is the love I have today.

My imperfect moment in time has suddenly become my perfect world.
If I could write the perfect ending to my imperfect story, my perfect world would end asleep in your sleeping arms.

If Only She Knew.......

Valerie D Wade

If only she knew
how her beauty radiates like a cheerful butterfly
Just fluttering closely for a quick hello

If only she knew how her upbeat aura transforms the mood of
a dismal day

If only she knew how much her polite sweetness
Is a treasured commodity on this earth

If only she knew that the recipient of her sincere friendship
reaps a unique reward

If only she knew that she is a beautiful, rare gem
worthy of a priceless appraisal

If only she knew that as she searches deep within her soul,
She will see the beauty and compassion of her awesome spirit

If only she knew that she is not to be defined by another's
attention or affection
But just by knowing that she is a delicate endangered flower of
which few are worthy

If only she knew that although seasons may come and go
Not to be discouraged by seeds carried by winds of deception
In search of a brief encounter

If only she knew that her spirit patiently ripens for transplantation with
A loving partner worthy of her love during the right season
Who will see the beauty that is you.....................
His Soulmate

Impromptu & Untitled

Tracie Elaine

Sitting in the winds of change
existing only, as my Mother would say,
but feeling the pull of brazen
pondering what could have been so many years ago
wondering if a lovely mockery might be possible
a twin crescent of fate perhaps
but then acknowledge my persistent immaturity....

what then becomes of a possibility or potential
to compliment great minds?
I venture to find what the result of this growth
could bloom
will living continue as the adamant downer it has
been,
or bloom into my favorite sunflower and guide my
newborn confidence?
A victory it could be, as long as my heart stays
big,
unfaltering to the wretched aura of earth........

Lilac Tree

Valerie D Wade

I'm like the Lilac Tree,
just basking in the shade
Shyly blooming all my buds,
and releasing a sweet bouquet

No one even notices me,
as I mingle among the crowd.
But their senses can't ignore,
my intoxicating invisible cloud.

Beautifully part of the background,
But drawing subtle attention my way
lavender flowers waft with the breeze
While my branches slightly sway

Yes, I'm like a Lilac Tree, beautiful,
delicate, and, free
Waiting for my southern knight
To come and rescue me

Bio of a Buttafly

Tracie Elaine

Take the grunge out of the antique strings
and you may play her soul's song

Raise the gourd of ancient cultures
& you may consume her way

Lay under the dreamcatchers in the sky
& you may embrace her destined flight

Swim the Great Lakes to the English Channel
& you may gaze upon her dreams

Roll your bones along the Earth
& you may capture her sorrow

Love completely for yin or yang
& you may be her soulmate....

Another Sunrise That Waits for Me

Valerie D. Wade

The shadow of an autumn sunrise dances slyly behind its cover, waiting for me to rescue it from another chilly night.

Leaving restful sleep behind, I hurry to my window for a southern view, and reminisce on my impending retirement.

I fling open my drapes to reveal another sweet sunrise casting an array of hues in the distance. An awesome reunion, that never disappoints unless subdued by dark clouds.

This morning holds a special meaning for me as I depart my employment. Fond memories envelope me as I recall how each proposal held promise.

I leave with no regrets, but look forward to a renewed freedom, and a sense of fulfillment. Fulfilled by lives that I have touched, and by those that have touched mine.

I look forward to the liberation that this change evokes, and approach the days ahead with much excitement. Unencumbered by responsibilities, but overflowing with imaginative possibilities.

As the sun sets on this special day, I savor the past and preview the potential that my new future holds while looking forward to keeping one appointment with…

…another sunrise that waits for me

Chapter 2

The Night

Sunshine

Toni M. Whitney

Oh, sunshine, how I long for you, Especially on these
cloudy days.
My SAD lamp tries its best, But it's just not the same, you
see.
You were the nectar of the Gods in a time gone by.
A guiding light through history!
Sunshine, you're so important to me,
You lift my spirits and make me feel free.
Your warmth on my skin, your light in my eyes,
the brightness you bring to the sky.
Sunshine, I need you desperately,
To keep my mind and body healthy.
So please shine down on me today,
And chase these dreary clouds away.

Jelly Beans

Tracie Elaine

A story about a stone woman made me think on it...
How to build a shield mocking thorns?
Where I can retreat, escape, or simply get lost
Lost into a chronically gutless void
Or maybe continue to try and balance the chaos, settling...
like what I've done all my life
Eating too many jellybeans
Breaking bread with mad lovers and toxic friends
Drinking too much rum & wine
Desperate to sink into the comfy seat of denial
Running in place, with toes heavy
The trap was set well, with all of our hands in it
Freedom will not come easy...

Did you think about me?

Toni M. Whitney

Did you think about me?
While we were apart.
Did I ever enter the chambers of your heart?
Did you think about me?
When summer turned to fall.
When winter was not far away.
Our favorite time of all!
Did you think about me?
In the spring when all things were new.
When the sun would rise
A new day for me and for you,
Or as the sunset
Our secrets cloaked in the dark
When we danced among the shadows
And whispered in the park?
Did you think about me?

The Paper

Valerie D Wade

It started out as just a tree
Standing in the woods alone
But now it's a piece of paper
Waiting for words unknown

Letters thrown together
Can really change a life
Sometimes it can be happy news
Sometimes it's added strife

I looked at this innocent envelope
That once was just a tree
I wish I hadn't opened it
It wasn't even addressed to me
It was an invitation
An unexpected piece of news
Someone was getting married
I suddenly got the blues

I didn't let those around me
Know the power that this paper held
I maintained my composure
Although I could have yelled

I could feel my face getting warm
as I climbed the endless stairs
Closing the door behind me
Hiding from my deep despair

My mind raced with many thoughts
How could I have been such a fool?
Is it a crime to love someone? I said
As my tears fell in a pool

An innocent piece of paper
That once was just a tree
Letters thrown together
Forever changing me

Love's Rain

By Robin E. Thorpe

Love's rain is a stream from the eyes of the crushed. Through agony and pain a heart that has ached too much.

Love's rain is a teardrop from a long and lonely night, shed upon a pillow's fluff; absorbed away from sight.

Love's rain is the pools of tears in the eyes of one whose heart has been broken, or the flooded cheeks from a wounded soul; whose words remain unspoken.

Love's rain is the endless weeping, longing for a loved one's touch. It is saying goodbye to a weary soul whose body had enough.

At the loss of true love, the tears will come to wash away the pain. Offering the cleansing comfort, from the downpour of love's rain.

Eyes Why Do You Wander?

By Robin E. Thorpe

Eyes, why do you wander? You know you must be brief.
Staying out there for too long won't bring your soul relief.
You'll find yourself out traveling far away from home.
Oh, eyes please gain some self-control; it isn't safe to roam!

Eyes, why do you wander? You'll cause your heart to stray,
Before you know it, you will find you've drifted far away.

Eyes, why do you wander? Just cover with your hand.
Hurry now, before you sink into your soul's quicksand.

Eyes, why do you wander? Remove that from your sight.
Careful or you'll ask yourself "How did I spend the night?

Eyes, why do you wander? Just simply turn around,
or you could be searching for yourself; never to be found.

Collar

Tracie Elaine

Dr. Phil can't help me; I don't need my head xamined.
It doesn't matter when the fear of being myself started; I
just need to get this collar off my neck.

I am sick
Sick of smiling when I feel haggard
Haggard from the aim to please
Pleasing everyone but one
One with a fire inside that would incinerate this 24/7 glee
club
Clubbed with the weight of playing the part
Playing dodge ball when anyone gets near
Nearly choking …

Chapter 3

Oh, Humanity

Palpable

Valerie D. Wade

..a knee on his neck
Palpable
..begging to breathe
Palpable
..calling for his Mother
Palpable
...losing consciousness
.life slipping away
Palpable
..no knock warrant
Palpable
..no justice for Breyonna
Palpable
...wails and cries of family
Palpable
...unspeakable grief
Palpable
..sounds of sirens
Palpable
...tears
Palpable
...anger
Palpable
..sounds of shattering glass
Palpable
...smell of smoke
Palpable
...marching

Palpable
...protesting
Palpable
...prayer
Palpable
..Remembrance
Palpable
...Saying their name
Palpable
...Never Forget
PALPABLE

Just Another Spray in the Hood

By Robin E. Thorpe

Where are you writer? I hope I can find you today, I've had so many distractions along the way.
Gunshots ringing out before the sunrise, it happens so often I'm not even surprised.

I still don't know who it was that lost their life today.
I just watched the police search for bullets that were sprayed.

It's so sad to think of the many times I've called, and the ones paid to protect us didn't show up at all.
I'm concerned that it could be the young woman who screams, was it her death that interrupted my dream?

I hope she was not the one for whom someone phoned, she has two babies who would be left alone.
I pray it wasn't her little one that caused our neighborhood to wake so alarmed.
It's even more painful when the innocent are harmed.

Perhaps it's the man who often made her cry and shout.
He'd return and beat on the door, after she put him out.

Could be that the police received the call, which had nothing to do with them at all?

Maybe someone else lost their life today, as warm, and snug in our beds the rest of us lay.

No tires screeched from a car speeding away, other than the
gunshots just a normal day.
If I had run to their rescue, could I have helped them? Wisdom
made me stay down and not become a victim.

I later stepped outside and what I found, was an empty quiet block
with no one around.

It appeared that nothing ever occurred, which should make us all feel
even more disturbed.

Unfortunately, many of us are desensitized, and world violence is
just a part of our everyday lives.

The Cloak of Covid-19
(4/10/2020)

Valerie D. Wade

This poem was reimagined from a poem written about the Oklahoma Bombing

It is hard to imagine the pain they must be feeling,
Not knowing where loved ones are, or even if they're breathing
Frantically ushered away from families in tears
Void of the outcome, heightening fears

Left alone in the hospital gasping for air,
Exhausted doctors and nurses providing their care
Relatives praying that the news will be good
Hang on a little longer if you could

Trapped in this nightmare, despair everywhere,
Trying to hold on while steeped in prayer

Some didn't make it, it happened so fast
Every age, race, and sex caught in the virus' path
The effort, the protocols, they just had to try,
But many succumbed without a proper goodbye

An epic pandemic, the world defined
Social distancing, they say will shorten the time

Through the madness human kindness gives glimmers of hope
Staying apart while trying to cope
When the plague has left us, and the healing starts
Lives will be changed forever
So many broken hearts.

Written in 2016

BEHIND EVERY HASHTAG

#nomorehashtags...

Valerie D. Wade

A nation of hashtags, is what we've become...
Behind every hashtag are endless memorials
Behind every hashtag is heartache and grief
Behind every hashtag is sadness
Behind every hashtag is loneliness
Behind every hashtag is anger
Behind every hashtag is confusion
Behind every hashtag is hopelessness
Behind every hashtag are unanswered questions
Behind every hashtag are endless tears
Behind every hashtag are endless prayers
Behind every hashtag is fear
Behind every hashtag are blood filled streets
Behind every hashtag is numbness
Behind every hashtag is a grieving family
Behind every hashtag are fatherless children
Behind every hashtag are childless Mothers
Behind every hashtag are Motherless children
They were just doing their job
They were just providing protection
They were just on their way
They were just going to work
They were just relocating to a new job
They were just hustling to make ends meet
They were just, they were Just, and they were just...

Black Lives,
Blue Lives
Your Life
My Life
ALL Lives….ALL Lives!
Beyond every hashtag is hope, healing, and a love that
surpasses it all
ALL OF OUR LIVES ARE SACRED AND OUR LIVES
MATTER

Because I'm Brown

By Robin E. Thorpe

A stranger to you I am.
You don't even know my name, but you hate me because I'm brown.
How is it that we've never spoken a single word to each other, yet you hate me because I'm brown?
You don't know that my heart is filled with kindness, and neither do you care; you simply hate me because I'm brown.
You'll never understand that you're mentioned in my prayers, which won't make one difference to you because you just hate me because I'm brown.
Someday you might find that you need help that I can provide and would ever so willingly give, if you allowed me into your life, but you can't because you hate me.
You hate me!
You don't hate me because I've done some horrible evil deed to you or your family or because I've destroyed something or someone you love.
At least that would be a valid reason.
You don't even know the reason you hate me; you only know that you've grown up being taught to hate me.
Yes, you just hate!
You just hate me!
It's such a shame that you hate me.
You just hate me because I'm brown.

YOUR LOSS!!!

Chapter 4

Love's Light

Desire

Toni M. Whitney

Roses are red
Violets are blue
It wasn't your eyes
That drew me
To you
It was those Oscar Robertson
Thighs.....
Hello!

Soulbirds

Tracie Elaine

That kiss still makes me blush!
I carry it with me, like a hidden bonus track
Along with the passport stamps your generous eardrops and
stimulating convos lend
Altogether illuminated by friendship, a bond like comrades,
unscathed by time...
Allow me to pay tribute with the trimmings of my weightless
imagination
To skinny dip along the emotive channels of our bond
Be they intellectually, artistically, or sexually charged
What we have is no threat to our other bridges,
For we capture an enviable understanding, with discrete
delight
Kindred soul birds tending the vibrant and timeless fire lily
between us....

Extraordinary

Tracie Elaine

Your eyes are stars and you embrace the Earth with your big
heart
the King of my thoughts, the inspiration of my bravest dreams
the joy that I have will burn always and with luck the future
will remain agreeable.
but this fire will survive either way and we will carry this
energy we share always
and so I thank you ahead of the unknown
because the present is so extraordinary & beautiful........

Man of Desire

By Robin E. Thorpe

Oh man of desire why do you remain as you are?
Have you spent too many years loving her from afar?

What is it about her that draws you so near?
Is it the sweetness of her voice that echoes in your ear?

What is the price that you are willing to pay for such a
treasure?
Are you ready to break your covenant, so that she can give you
pleasure?

What is it about her beauty that leaves you mesmerized?
Will you forsake it all, for the love you fantasize?

Oh man of desire, is she worth it all?
Effortlessly seducing, as you remain enthralled?

Perhaps you should comb carefully through those blades of
green.
Searching for thorns and other dangers unforeseen.

Is time spent holding her really worth the price you'll pay?
For your last moments on earth, are her arms where you
would stay?

Oh man of desire, please consider carefully.
Will loving her change the outcome of your destiny?

How long will you wait to hold on to her so tight?
Is she honestly worth the effort to be your delight?

Beware man of desire, of what her presence brings.
Moving too fast in her direction could cost you everything.

Long Island Ice Tea

Tracie Elaine

I'm crazy 'bout you baby -so, don't hold back
Let's dive into the ocean of
Long Island Ice Teas
We can be happily intoxicated moment to moment
No need to dwell on a single day past
Right here, right now
Enthusiasm ahead

I bask in your attention
As you are tickled by the safeguard I manage,
despite the wonderful emotions you tap into
Sweet concertos your fingers play
in ode to a hopeless romantic

You are my muse and I your kitten
Are we now official valentines?
Let this revue mark time
& tally tickets around the world

Shall we explore the Milky Way of sensuality?
Tuning an enviable melody
in creative companionship

I'm crazy 'bout you baby
So, let's enjoy this joy
& cherish our new freedom in each
other's eyes. ...

Sundae

Tracie Elaine

Energy
Nonstop
till we dropped...
my thighs played a sweet melody
as my hips forgot the blues
and began to scat, scat, scat...
like Nina Simone making love
to a bittersweet ballad
Routine escaped me and my favorite muse,
as we dove into the seduction of a neo smorgasbord
where rhythm hippies and free spirits swapped
positive vibes
fearlessly harmonious in the sweet retreat
of a techno sundae..

Autumn Love

By Robin E. Thorpe

Alone I sit and watch as the sun glistens its reflections on the tiny
ripples of water.
I gaze at the sky with birds soaring about fluttering their wings, and I
think of you.
My heart yearns to see the sunset in your warm brown eyes.
I can almost feel you wrap your strong arms around me as we stand
on the shore.
Your embrace protects me from the autumn chill.
Faint smiles of bliss decorate our faces.
Cheek to cheek we sway in the gentle breeze.
For we have kissed summer's evenings goodbye.
Later we will share our evening's delights under the watchful eye of
the full harvest moon.

Please

By Robin E. Thorpe

Please come
Please warm
Please touch
Please hold
Please kiss
Please squeeze
Please soothe
Please stroke
Please love
Please come, warm, touch, hold, kiss, squeeze, soothe, stroke, love
me
and please repeat!!!

Embracing Your Love

By Robin E. Thorpe

That warm breeze blew you into my life and ushered you straight
into my heart.
A natural charismatic whirlwind seems to surround you and keep my
heart locked in all these years.
I don't even want to imagine being in the world without seeing that
glimmer your eyes hold just for me.
How wonderful it is to remain in that extra special place in your soul.
I welcome it all with an invisible shield placed around me.
How could I have known that our first moments glance would last a
lifetime.
I have chosen to embrace your love.

Unspoken Melody

By Robin E. Thorpe

When I lay my head upon your chest, I know that everything
is alright.
I bask in the strength of your sweet caress, as you hold me
ever so tight.

Whatever happened in my day that went wrong, no longer
matters to me.
I'm enfolded in your loving arms, so strong, where I can
unwind and be free.

Hearing your heartbeat is what I long to do, every time that I
have you near.
It seems to say, "I love you, and I will always be right here."

The warmth of your body feels so sweet; it soothes my very
soul.
I'm mesmerized by its heat, as it welcomes me in from the
cold.

Laying my head on your chest are precious moments that I
hold dear.
I can rest secure in our intimate hours, as your heart beats in
my ear.

I know the melody that it plays is in perfect rhythm with
mine,
and I cuddle up at the end of my day; thanking God it's your
heartbeat I find.

A Visit from Paradise

Valerie D. Wade

Close your eyes and imagine this…

A clear blue beautiful sky, not a cloud in sight
The warmth of sunshine caresses your face
The melody of chirping birds elevates your mood

A modest whisper of wind blowing…A fragile breeze
Grass as green as a new crayon, the crisp fresh air calms you

Can you feel it….

Children laughing and playing, singing their songs
Sounds of a brand-new summer day, just moseying along

As sundown nears, a stillness fills the air
A bronze hue casts over the heavens,
as the sun fades into the background
Dusk falls lightly over the scene

Darkness subtlety creeps down in a slow lull,
Soon the night sky is imminent
Bright stars shine like carefully sprinkled diamonds
An ever so slight breeze cools the air
The melody of crickets echoes everywhere
Specks of fireflies here and there
A blissful evening has set in…

A relaxing spirit takes over as an indescribable
Fulfillment is realized
…you savor another enchanting visit from…..Paradise

Chapter 5

Letters

I'll Wait for You

By Marie Braithwaite Sherman Batchelor

This evening when the sun goes down and skies are red and blue, I shall be left with all the dreams I ever shared with you.

I'll be thinking of the night we kissed and said goodbye, and how we had to part without the time to wonder why.

I shall remember all you said, and I shall tell myself. These things must linger many months upon my lonely shelf.

But I shall wait with all my heart, however far away. To hold you in my arms again, whatever be the day, and surely every hour will be more than worth the while,

If only we shall meet again, and I shall see your smile.

For Aida

By Robin E. Thorpe

Sister, I can't tell you how many times I sat and thought of you.
Wondering if you were alright and what kinds of things you like to
do.

For years I longed to see your face and was curious about your life.
I didn't know if you were a Mother, or some fine gentleman's wife.

I would look at your baby pictures knowing you were connected to
me,
However, your location was one big mystery.

I always knew another girl out there had a piece of Daddy's heart.
I understood that he loved you even though you were far apart.

We talked about finding you someday but didn't know where to
begin.
I believe that each of us always carried you somewhere deep within.

I'm so thankful to God for finally completing our family.
I can see daddy smiling from Heaven saying that's where my
daughter should be.

Aida Thomas

Missing Daddy

Valerie D. Wade

*Dedicated to my Daddy, **James William Sherman** – 1931-1996
and to all those missing their Daddy*

My Daddy left us just three months ago
There's not a day that passes, that I don't miss him so

Whenever I turn the corner and see his empty chair
I can't erase the feeling that he should be sitting there

Thoughts of him flow through me at moments in my day
I always feel his presence when I begin to pray

Still numb from the reality that he is really gone
But cherishing his memory since he has passed on

He used to kiss us on the forehead,
as he would leave for work each day

And when he would return each night
he would stand at his Bible and pray

He loved to visit parks on hot summer days
Just lying on a blanket and soaking up the rays

I'll never forget the things I learned from him
as a child, and then an adult
Just following his example and remembering the love I felt

Things have changed so much since he has gone away
A void that can never be filled
A heart that aches each day

Although the pain never goes away
The ache gets duller with time
I've learned to focus on the memories
and leave the hurt behind

Papa

By Valerie D. Wade

Rupert Eugene Braithwaite

He remembers back when he was young
When he was just a lad
He even recalls the songs that he's sung
While back in Trinidad

He was the youngest of the Braithwaite clan
And even a twin to boot
He's a trustworthy and honest man
Awfully handsome in a suit

He's quite the gentleman you will see
Polite in every way
He enjoys sharing a story with you and me
Just about any day

His memory is as sharp as a tack
He recalls as the closes his eyes
The stories they go way back
At the end there's always a surprise

The cats they all gather to meet him
Waiting anxiously for the day's feast
They know he won't disappoint them
Even in weather fit for neither man nor beast

They gobble their food and then scatter
Going on their merry way
With their tummies all full and fatter
To start out another day

He always enjoys cooking and baking
In his spice rack you're sure to find curry
A cake in the oven he's making
If he promised you one, not to worry

He likes to drink his coffee strong
Hot as it can get
He hasn't forgotten a romantic song
Or even the people he's met

In his garden he used to spend hours
A pleasant scent to behold
Tending carefully to his flowers
Or possibly a green rose

You can find him listening to the baseball game
In hopes that they will win
You know he will always be the same
You can always count on him

He is proud of all of his grands
I am blessed to be one of them
He has held each of us in his hands
And he knows that we all love him

Daddy

Toni M. Whitney

Daddy, how I miss you when I watch politics today,
Your commentary and insights, your passion for debate.
I would take the opposite side, with fervor and with glee, We could
go at it for hours ... .
But when you pulled down your glasses to the brim of your nose
I knew our debate had come to a close .
You taught me to think critically, to question the status quo, To
stand up for what I believe in,
even if I'm alone. You showed me the power of words, and the
importance of fighting for
what's right, Even when it's difficult, even when it's a fight.
Now that you're gone, I'm a ship without a sail,
Lost in a sea of opinions, without your details.
But I know that you're still with me, in my heart and in my mind.
Sometimes I hear your voice coming from me
when I say what's on my mind!
As I watch the politicians on TV, bickering and squabbling,
I wonder if you would have gotten cable so you could switch back
and forth or would you be so fed up you that you had switched to
sports!.Thank you, Dad, for everything. I miss you more than words
can say

James William Sherman

Papa's Garden

Tracie Elaine

I can still hear the wheels of the reel mower turning those gigantic
blades, and yielding a perfect blanket of freshly cut grass

The smell of that fresh cut, bordered by a radiant variety of
flowers, with hostas galore and colorful marigolds.

Don't forget the grapes!
A bountiful macrame of sweet and sour
Some to wash for lunch or dinner
Some rationed away to make wine
Some simply plucked and eaten right off the stem

Wonderful memories collected as a helper,
bagging the grass, and once tall enough, pushing the mower.
Student and daydreamer spoiled by the beautiful view

An adored bar set for generations,
nurtured with pride and a love of nature's beauty

Loss

Toni M. Whitney

Within a year, my world was torn apart, My only brother and
youngest sister, gone.
My heart is heavy, my soul is bare,
I cannot comprehend this pain and despair.
My brother, my confidant, my rock, He was our go to for all things
spiritual
He was the glue that held us together. .
He always knew what to say and how to say it.
My sister, my sunshine, my memory keeper.
She knew birthdays, anniversaries, and deaths in that order!
I miss their laughter, their love, their embrace, Their warm smiles,
the ease with which they spoke to strangers
who they would soon add to our clan.
I long to hear their voices again,
But all that remains are echoes in my mind.

Kris Jeanne Sherman-Burns and William Emanual Sherman

To Frida Kahlo

Tracie Elaine

Many find despair in your story
but I gather courage
along the path to lose all excuses
it is impossible to justify hiding in the shadows
How many trains would I miss,
if never to know your journey
and the paths of many sisters that would not be silenced
or restrained
I gather courage in your story
where many find despair
along the shore my inhibitions dissolve
and whisper goodbye in the wind
As life guarantees nothing,
I can seize the minutes with brazen expression
alive without the world's conditional consent
Staying free to carry the spirit you ignited so many moons
ago........

Ever Present

By Robin E. Thorpe

You held me in your hands, when I was filled with fear, giving
constant reassurance that you are always near.
No matter what the circumstance my life has led me to, I can walk in
faith and trust that you'll be there to see me through.
Life's imperfect journey is often filled with trials, but I'm sure that
you are with me, even in my crooked miles.
I'm certain that there are times when I've disappointed you, and
although I've had my failures, you have come to pull me through.
I know that I should never worry about what this life may bring, for
you are ever with me throughout everything.

Just Feelings

By Robin Thorpe

God, I feel so abandoned; yet I know that you never leave me or forsake me.

I'm feeling lost, but I know you've found me.

I feel bound up, and you've already given me liberty.

I feel sad Lord, but you gave me your joy.

My soul seems a bit troubled, however you've given me your perfect peace.

Lord, I feel so defeated!!! Yet, victory is mine.

I feel so rejected Lord, but I have your unconditional love.

Thank you, Lord that salvation is mine.

Know that I am at Peace!

By Robin E. Thorpe

I hear your cries and see your tears and those you must release.
and if by chance you are wondering, please know that I am at peace.

If somehow, you have known me and been part of my life.
Cry if you must but not for me, I'm all done with stress and strife.

You see I have journeyed to this place and found my body is new.
No more pain and suffering, I am smiling and waiting for you.

I made my choice years ago to let the Lord have me.
I am not at all worried about where I will spend my eternity.

I am absent from that tired body and present with the Lord.
Standing now before him waiting for my reward

Please do not fret and focus on things that I went through.
Take time now to prepare your spirit so you can come here too.

You will never understand all the reasons I had to depart.
Just know that I am with my savior and peace is in my heart.

Chapter 6

Dawn

Fulfilled

By Robin E. Thorpe

Please knock before entering my heart! You need my permission, right?
Did I willingly give it without knowing? Did I unwillingly surrender my heart?

What am I supposed to do now that you have moved in?
You set up residence!
You made yourself comfortable, just laying around everywhere, and swallowing up every crumb!

Yes, you are guilty of hanging your sign, in bold print, which reads "OCCUPIED!!!"
How dare you fill every shelf and overstuff every closet and drawer!
You didn't leave a space anywhere!

There is not even a tiny crack for someone else to fill.
How dare you!!!
Really!
How dare you love and fulfill me so much, that I don't have room enough to receive anymore!

I guess I'll just embrace it.
I tried but I can't shake it.

One name!
One aim!
One love!

I do, however, have ONE thing to say.

Thank you!

Should I

By Robin E. Thorpe

Should I behold the highest mountain or wander in the lowest valley.
Should I swim in the deepest ocean or fly amongst the clouds in the sky.
Should I touch the purest gold, or behold this earth's paradise, and fail to see you face to face.
I have done, seen, felt, or been nothing.
My very existence would be pointless, if I have never known you, my Lord!
My every breath would be wasted.
Life really has no meaning, without the knowledge of you.

Lord How You Love Me

By Robin E. Thorpe

Lord how you love me, as only you can.
For this is truly Heaven sent, above that of a man.

Every hair upon my head, mysteriously you see.
I inhale and exhale with the breath you've given me.

Lord, how you love me in your very special way.
You guide me with your wisdom, to help me through each day.

Lord how you love me, as I drift off to sleep.
I'm sure to slumber peacefully; knowing me you'll keep.

Whenever I'm in trouble, you send Angels to protect.
You even accept parts of me that others would reject.

Somehow, wherever I may be, you see my falling tears.
I'm certain that you'll be with me throughout all of my years.

Rest

By Robin E. Thorpe

Girl, do you even know how to rest?
You need to learn how to make yourself de-stress.

You lie down at night all cozy in your bed, but now you need to clear
your head.
Thoughts are running all over the place, but no one would know by
the look on your face.

You appear to be resting so peacefully, but your mind isn't resting,
it's too busy.

It's so lost in thought about what tomorrow brings and caught up
entertaining all kinds of things.

Don't you wish you could simply turn every thought away, and truly
rest as down in bed you lay?

There is a solution to your problem, and you know where to look.
It's found among the promises of that precious book.

Chapter 7

Tell Me a Story – A Gathering of Short Stories

A Visit With Papa

Valerie D. Wade

As I open the front door and step into the living room, the pungent scent of curry welcomes me. *Papa must be making curry chicken*, I thought. The scent of curry permeates the walls of this small dwelling from several decades of preparing curry dishes. *He will curry me if I stand still*, I laugh to myself. I hang my trench coat on the antique coat rack behind the front door.

"Valerie, is that you?" he calls from the kitchen in his thick Trinidadian accent.

"Yes, it's me, Papa.'"

I hear Papa shuffling across the worn tiled kitchen floor clanging pots and pans, running water, and serving up food simultaneously. In the background, I can hear the voice of Ernie Harwell narrating the Tigers baseball game. As I am just about to enter the kitchen to see what I can do to help, Papa comes out carrying a full serving of curry chicken and rice, covered with curry juice and green peppers, with a side of green beans. My mouth waters at the site of this familiar dish. His wavy silver hair is neatly in place as always, his shirt is tucked in his pants, and is buttoned to the neck with his long underwear top peeking out just under his neck, and he is wearing his black leather slippers that cover his heels.

I scoot up to the place setting that is waiting for me and remain quiet because I know the protocol; Papa is in charge, and will refuse my help, in fact, he considers it an insult.

"Thanks, Papa."

I can feel the roughness of his scruffy gray beard as he kisses my cheek and heads quickly back to the kitchen. I smile because I know that there is only one thing missing, and I look up as he hands me a cold glass of Vernors Ginger Ale.

"Enjoy!" he says as he goes back to the kitchen to finish washing dishes.

The bubbles tickle my nose as I take my first sip of Vernors. This is the only thing that Papa ever serves. Every forkful brings back memories from my childhood. *None of us can make curry chicken like Papa*, I thought. I contemplate as I eat, what he would say if he knew that I substitute ketchup for real tomatoes, when I make this dish. *This is how my Mother taught me to make it*, I think as I savor the last few bites.

As I bring my clean plate back to the kitchen, and try to wash it myself, Papa gives me a familiar glance. I smile and quickly hand the dish over to him, and head back to my seat. When I think that I am unable to eat another thing, I find that I can't refuse a slice of his lemon pound cake. Upon finishing my cake, Papa quickly hurries me out of the door with a generous hug. I inhale the strong scent of tobacco from his Marlboro cigarette that he is holding, with the ashes so long that they just about fall to the floor.

"I know you worked all day, so get home before it is dark." he says. I am thankful for you working people to keep my Social Security coming in." he exclaims with a hearty laugh.

Fresh Flowers

By Robin E. Thorpe

Alexandra turned up the volume, hoping to soothe herself, with the sound of her favorite jazz artist. She loved her job but hated the evening commute home. She often considered selling her home and purchasing one closer to her job. Naturally, she was tired at the end of her workday, but the evening traffic jam seemed to take whatever strength she had left. She sighed with relief as she turned into her driveway and waited for the sluggish garage door to open. When she was inside of the house, she quickly kicked off her black leather pumps, and made her way down the long corridor and entered her Mother's bedroom. No matter how sunny the day was; the room always seemed so dark. Lights could not change her broken heart. The thought of her Mother dying was always at the forefront of her mind. She looked down at her Mother lying there asleep as she placed her purse and keys on the bedside table.

"How is she today, Pat?" she asked the nurse who sat in the rocking chair near the window.

"About the same!" was all Pat could say.

Alexandra noticed the sadness in her eyes. It became all too familiar. She understood. Pat was very fond of her Mother and had taken care of her for nearly a year. She spent several years working in Hospice and told Alexandra it was always difficult to watch a patient slip away. The bond she formed with Mrs. Douglass and Alexandra was beyond professional. They had become her family.

Pat was Jamaican born and became an American citizen a few years back. Her only family was her Mother, who passed away ten years prior to her moving to the states. She made several friends but explained no one had ever been as close to her as the Douglass family. Pat and Alexandra understood that Mrs. Douglass was living out her last days. Pat shared with Alexandra the changes that would occur as the disease progressed, and she understood the final stage was not far off. Alexandra was grateful that Pat was available to stay with her Mother during the day, which allowed her to continue to maintain a sense of normalcy in her life. She chose to continue teaching her preschoolers; whom she referred to as her babies.

At age 43 she never married, nor had children, but dedicated her life to educating her little ones. A few years passed since she watched her Mother struggle to care for her father during his illness. She was amazed by the courage and strength that she saw in her. However, she never anticipated following her father's death, her Mother would become ill and totally dependent upon her. She was the only child of Mr. and Mrs. Alexander Douglass; No sibling to share the responsibility of caring for her Mother. Pat was a true blessing to her. A sudden stroke and cancer really took its toll on her Mother. Alexandra watched her go from vibrant, to almost skeletal and feeble. It was hard for her to see her Mother lying there motionless. She clearly understood that the peaceful expression she wore was only a mask. Every night, Alexandra shed silent tears at the thought of her Mother's pain. She often questioned God about her illness. She simply could not understand how a person who devoted her entire life to helping others, could end up in her condition.

Mrs. Douglass created a nonprofit to assist single Mothers with housing, shelter, food, and medical expenses. She also volunteered as a server in the neighborhood soup kitchens, and often donated money to several charities. Prior to her illness, she was often selected to sing solos in the choir at her church. Many times, Alexandra would hear remarks from others about her Mother's angelic voice. She reflected on the days when her mother spent hours tending to her beautiful garden, where she grew flowers of every kind. People frequently stopped and admired their beauty. Her heart was filled with regret about moving her Mother in to live with her. She never wanted to remove her from the comfort and familiar surroundings that their family home provided, however, driving three hours to work every day did not seem to be the best solution either.

To help relieve her stress Alexandra showered, as Pat checked her Mother's vital signs and injected her with a little dose of comfort. When she returned, Pat had gathered her things and was heading for the door.

"See you in the morning!" She whispered before closing it behind her.

"Alex!" Mrs. Douglass' raspy voice sounded.

"Hi, Mama!" Alexandra lovingly spoke, offering a warm smile as she entered her Mother's room.

Her Mother often spoke of her beautiful eyes and smile. Alexandra gently kissed her on the cheek and held her hand.

"Can I get you something, Mama?" She considered it an honor to provide whatever
comfort she could.

"Fresh flowers!" were the only words Mrs. Douglass uttered before drifting off to sleep again.

"I'll get you some tomorrow. I promise Mama!"

Alexandra glanced at the vase sitting on the windowsill. Every flower of the beautiful bouquet had begun to bow its head. The leaves were withered and dried. She thought about what the flowers meant to her Mother. Fresh flowers always gave her hope.

"New life!" is what her Mother would say when she noticed a new leaf, or flower bud in her garden.

The next day Alexandra remained in the classroom after all the students were dismissed. A few of the children suddenly became ill.

"High fevers, and vomiting! I need to disinfect this room! I cannot afford to get sick, and the last thing Mama needs is a virus!" She mumbled.

She scrubbed, wiped, and sprayed until she glanced at the clock. Although it didn't seem late, it was 4:45.

"Oh no! The florist closes at 5:00! I promised Mama fresh flowers! "

After locking the classroom door, she rushed out of the building and across the parking lot to her black Jeep, and quickly climbed inside. The tires screeched as she darted in and out of traffic, until she made a quick turn into the parking lot of Steve's Flowers. She leaped from the vehicle, almost forgetting to grab her keys as she ran to the door. When she approached, a young woman flipped the sign from open to closed.

"Oh no! Please! I will only be a minute!" Her frantic speech announced the desperation in her heart.

"Sorry Ma'am! But we're closed!" The young woman spoke through the closed glass door. "Please!" Alexandra pleaded.

"We're closed! You need to come back tomorrow morning! We open at 8:30!"

Alexandra sighed with frustration. Tears filled her eyes as she walked back to her Jeep. The last thing she wanted to do was disappoint her Mother. Suddenly, she heard a man's voice calling out to her.

"Excuse me! Would you like a bouquet of fresh flowers?" Alexandra turned to face him.

"Yes! How did you know?"

The sound of surprise was in her voice. She smiled at the handsome gentleman, who stood before her. She admired the way the sunlight glistened in his eyes, and added tiny sparkles to his graying temples, and moustache. She also took notice of his muscular frame. The green apron he wore only hid part of his bulging pectoral muscles. Also, the rolled-up sleeves of his white shirt revealed the trails created by the veins of his hairy forearms.

"I'm Steve! I noticed that you come in every week, and you always get a mixed bouquet of fresh flowers!"

"Steve! So, you must be the owner!" she softly spoke.

"I am! Now will you please come in and select the bouquet you would like?"

Steve held the door with one hand as he gestured to her with the other to come inside. A sudden north wind embraced Alexandra's body, creating chill bumps on her arms. She hunched her shoulders and used her hands to rub them away, as she walked quickly but carefully toward Steve.

"I know its spring, but sometimes these evening breezes really give me a chill!"

"It's always best to keep a jacket handy at this time of year. Steve advised.

"I do, but I was in a hurry, so I left it in the truck!"

Alexandra spoke though clenched teeth as she entered the fragrant shop.

"I won't be long! I really appreciate you allowing me to come in! I know you're closed for the day! Thank you, Steve!" Steve closed and locked the door behind her.

"Do I need to stay? I need to catch my bus!" the young woman snapped, as she put on her denim jacket.

A look of frustration was on her face, as she stood leering at Alexandra.

"No! You can go Shondra! I will take care of this lady! Good night!" Steve kindly spoke.

"Good night!" Shondra replied, as she charged out of the door.

Alexandra and Steve laughed at the way she power walked to the bus stop. Her hips quickly shifted from side to side in her faded jeans. She was careful to avoid the cracks between the concrete slabs with the spiked heels of her short black boots. Steve turned to face Alexandra once again, offering her a warm smile.

"Please select the bouquet you would like!"

Alexandra struggled as she tried not to stare at Steve. She thought he was quite handsome and was delighted by his chivalry. She quickly turned away and stood before the lighted display case.

Momentarily she gazed at the array of beautiful bouquets.

"The one with the baby's breath please!" She pointed to the far end of the top shelf.

"I knew you'd like that one!" Steve confidently spoke. Alexandra was surprised by his

words.

"How'd you know?"

"Most women like the baby's breath!"

Alexandra liked the way he smiled at her and returned one to him before she spoke.

"My Mother always said that the flowers are tiny, and sweet like a newborn baby!"

She watched as Steve removed the bouquet from the display case and tied a bright yellow ribbon around it.

"Just adding a little sunshine!" he said.

It seemed as if only moments had gone by. But the two of them lost themselves in conversation for nearly an hour and discovered they shared common interests. Steve was also caring for his ailing Mother. Alexandra glimpsed at the clock on the wall.

"I better get to Mama! It's almost time for the nurse to leave! I have enjoyed talking with you, Steve!" Her eyes twinkled as she spoke.

"Likewise! May I escort you to your car?" He stared deep into her eyes as he handed her the bouquet.

"Yes, I would like that! Thank you!" She loved being in the presence of a gentleman.

Alexandra turned to face the door, but suddenly spun around nearly bumping Steve with the bouquet.

"I'm sorry Steve" she spoke, as she scrambled through her small brown leather purse, and pulled out her credit card attempting to hand it to him. "I forgot to pay you!"

"This one is on me! Just get it home safely, without hitting anyone with it!" he teased.

The two of them laughed, and exchanged a few more pleasantries, before Alexandra backed out of the parking space, and made her exit into the flow of traffic. The following afternoon Alexandra dismissed her babies and made her way to the office.

"Miss Douglass!" The Secretary called to her as she entered.

Several faculty members stood around. Alexandra noticed the slight grins that were all about the room. All eyes were focused on her.

"I have a special delivery for you, from Steve's Flowers!" The secretary gave a slight grin and giggle.

Alexandra also heard whispers, and giggles behind her, as she approached the counter.

"Thank you, Miss Jacobs!" She blushed as she reached for the flowers.

"This is yours too!" Miss Jacobs added; snickering, as she handed Alexandra a single long-stemmed red rose.

Attached to it was a white ribbon that read: 4 U! HAVE A BEAUTIFUL DAY! BEAUTIFUL LADY! Alexandra carefully lifted the petals to her nose and inhaled their scent.

"Mmmm!" she moaned, as she closed her eyes and smiled.

"It must be from someone special!" Miss Jacobs teased.

Alexandra offered no explanation, but simply smiled and made her exit. Every Friday for the next month, she received a small bouquet of assorted flowers, and her rose. A message of encouragement or comfort scripture was always attached to each of them.

On the first day of the following month, she received her usual flowers but noticed a small card attached; inserted between the flowers of the bouquet.

Beautiful Alexandra,
I know you can't get away for dinner,
But will you join me for lunch tomorrow?
My treat!
Please call if you would like to accept my invitation.
With warm regards,
Steve

Alexandra was hesitant at first. It had been many years since she allowed herself to get involved in a relationship with a man. She was quite busy with her students, and her ailing Mother. It didn't seem to be the right time; however, Steve had been a comfort to her. She reflected on their former conversation. He certainly was someone who understood what she was going through.

His wonderful sense of humor and compassion was a delight to be around. She graciously accepted his invitation and joined him for lunch the following afternoon.

The two of them met at a small diner near the school. Steve pulled his black Jaguar into a space beside Alexandra's Jeep. She sat admiring the way he confidently walked as he approached her door to open it. She also loved the way the tiny lines formed at the corner of his warm brown eyes as he smiled. She thought of how perfect his eyes seemed to be with his bronze complexion. He greeted her with a fresh bouquet, and her rose. Alexandra thanked him and gently placed them in the passenger seat before they went inside to dine. The two of them enjoyed lunch with laughter and friendly conversation. It had been quite a while since she felt that way.

"I hope you'll join me again soon!" Steve requested, as he escorted her back to her Jeep.

"Thanks for inviting me! I really enjoyed it." Her eyes showed the sincerity of her words.

"My pleasure! I'm glad that you were able to join me."

He opened her door and waited until she was seated.

"I know its short notice Alexandra, but will you join me tomorrow, at the same time and place?"

Her heart fluttered with excitement.

"Yes! I am looking forward to it!"

Alexandra drove home that evening, reflecting on her lunch date with Steve. She could not hide her happy expression as she entered her Mother's room.

"Alex, you look happy!" Mrs. Douglass spoke softly, as she noticed Alexandra's bright smile.

"Did you meet someone special?"

Her daughter had not worn that expression in years, but Mrs. Douglass knew it well.

"Yes Mama! He is special! His name is Steve!"

Alexandra spent the evening telling her Mother all about Steve.

"Sounds like God sent you an Angel!" Mrs. Douglass' speech slurred a bit as she drifted off to sleep.

The next morning Alexandra received her usual flowers. She removed the tiny envelope and pulled out the card. She quickly shoved it back inside when she noticed another teacher approaching.

"Good morning, Miss Douglass!" He kindly spoke as he quickly walked past.

She returned the greeting and made her way down the long corridor to her classroom. When she was safely inside, she closed the door and stood beside her desk. Her heart fluttered with excitement. She was curious about Steve's message and knew that she only had a few moments alone before the children would arrive. Her hands nervously trembled as she removed the card once again.

Beautiful Alexandra,
Thank you for joining me for lunch yesterday.
I was looking forward to dining with you today, however,
the passing of my Mother last night leads me to
making final arrangements today.

Let's postpone it until Monday.
Steve

Sadness suddenly gripped her as she thought about what Steve must have been going through.

Alexandra called and offered her condolences to him that evening. The two of them met for lunch the following Monday. Steve shared his plans for a Memorial service on Saturday morning. Several relatives were expected to arrive in town for the service.

"I know it may be difficult or maybe impossible for you to join me, but it would really be a comfort to me if I could see your smile there!" Steve spoke.

Alexandra wanted to honor his request, and asked Pat to sit with her Mother that morning and allow her to be with him during his time of sorrow. Without hesitation, Pat agreed.

Alexandra arrived at the church Saturday morning. Few seats were available, so she sat quietly on the back pew. When the service was over Steve began to move around, greeting relatives and friends. Alexandra made her way to the front of the church where he stood. Steve noticed her approaching. He smiled as he reached for her hand.

"Alexandra! Thank you for coming! As always, it is a pleasure to see you!"

He gently kissed her on the cheek.

"I'm glad that I was able to be here. Pat is with Mama."

Steve took Alexandra all around the church introducing her to his relatives and friends.

"Alexandra this is my brother Pete! Be careful! He's a sly one!" Steve warned.

Pete seemed to devour Alexandra with his hazel eyes; making her feel uncomfortable, as he kissed her hand.

"Alexandra I've heard a lot about you. You are every bit as beautiful as Steve said you were!"

"Thank you!" She said blushing, as Pete lifted her hand to his lips for a second kiss.

He stared into her eyes.

"Come on Alexandra! There is someone else I want you to meet!"

Steve quickly took her hand and moved her away from Pete, and over to where his Aunt Emily sat alone in the front pew. Emily smiled as the two of them approached.

"You must be Alexandra?" Emily surprised her as she spoke.

"Yes!" Alexandra quickly responded. Steve introduced the two of them.

"It's nice to meet you!" Alexandra said, smiling, as Emily stood to embrace her.

She noticed the strong family resemblance. She admired how classy Emily looked in her blue suit, and fancy matching hat with the tiny silver flowers, and jewelry. *Not even the queen of England is more elegant than this lady.* she thought.

"I've heard all about you!" Emily proudly announced, smiling back at Alexandra.

"Really!" The sound of surprise was in her voice.

She was uncertain about Steve's feelings for her but was unexpectedly delighted by the brief conversation she shared with Emily. The two of them sat and talked as Steve went about greeting the other guests.

"Steve has always been like a son to me. His Mother and I were sisters, and we have always been close. I never had children, so she shared her boys with me!" Emily explained.

Alexandra was surprised at how much Steve told his aunt about her.

"I've never seen that man's face light up the way it does when he talks about you!" she continued.

Alexandra wanted to stay and talk with Emily further, but she had only asked Pat to stay for a short time. She did not want to take advantage of a friend who had become so dear to her.

"I really enjoyed talking to you, but I need to get home to my Mother. The nurse doesn't usually come on Saturday, so I don't want to keep her too long!"

"I understand! You and Steve are good children, taking care of your Mothers that way!

I hope to see you again soon, Alexandra! Steve can bring you by the house sometime!"

Emily's voice was warm and inviting, as she embraced Alexandra once more. Steve approached and offered to escort Alexandra out. She was anxious to get Steve outside alone for a few moments.

"I hear you've been talking a lot about me!"

"I can't deny that!" Steve was proud to say.

Alexandra couldn't hide her joyful expression.

"Your Aunt Emily seems very sweet. She said you are like a son to her."

"That is true! My Mother and Aunt Emily were together nearly every day when I was growing up. When Mother became ill, she still came around every day. Even when Mother stopped talking a year ago! She has always been there for us. It has been like having two Mothers!"

"I would love to meet with you for lunch Monday, if you're free Alexandra!"

"Same time, and place?" she asked.

"Just as long as it's alright with you!"

"That will be perfect!"

"May I call you this evening, Alexandra?"

"I would love that Steve, but you should spend time with your family while they're in town!"

"I'm sure you're right. Thank you for being so thoughtful! That's one of the things I love about you, Alexandra!"

"Really! Do you have a list?"

"Yes, and it's growing!"

"That's great!" Alexandra couldn't hide her blushing face.

"Tell me Alexandra, do you also have a list?"

She remained silent and simply smiled at Steve as she drove away.

Several weeks went by as Alexandra and Steve continued to share lunch at least three days a week. The two of them talked every evening before she went to sleep, and Steve continued to send fresh flowers. Her classroom always had a pleasant fragrance, which her students loved, and her Mother was tickled by the tiny bouquets she brought home. One evening as Alexandra returned from work, she was pleasantly surprised by her Mother. Mrs. Douglass unexpectedly requested a meeting with Steve, and he agreed to meet with her. They planned it for the following Sunday afternoon.

When he arrived at the Douglass residence, Alexandra greeted him with a tender embrace.

She loved the way his black suit was wearing him but was mesmerized by the masculine fragrance he wore. The two of them had become quite close, and she loved every moment of being in his presence.

"Excuse me, Steve; I'm going to let Mama know that you're here!"

"Of course!"

Steve sat and admired the beautiful vases that decorated the living room. Alexandra quickly returned and noticed.

. "Mom's collection is impressive, isn't it?"

"It certainly is! I only wish that I had met her sooner. I could have used her help in selecting a few pieces for the shop!"

"Come on, she's ready to see you now!"

Steve followed Alexandra into her Mother's bedroom. He slowly approached her bedside.

"Hello Mrs. Douglass! I have been looking forward to meeting you!"

"Likewise, Steve! Thank you for making my baby so happy!"

Her voice was low and raspy, but Steve understood every word.

"I'm glad to do it! She has been my sunshine too!" He lovingly smiled at Alexandra.

Alexandra could not hide her delightful expression, and quickly excused herself to make tea for the three of them. She soon returned, placing the tray on the bedside table.

"Have the two of you been having a good visit? "

"Yes baby! Very nice!" Mrs. Douglass whispered.

Alexandra's heart fluttered when she noticed tears on her Mother's face.

"Mama you've been crying!"

"Yes baby! Happy tears!"

"What's going on, Mama? "

"Alexandra! Why don't you come and sit beside your Mother!" Steve requested, as he offered her his chair.

He noticed the way Alexandra trembled a bit, but kept a fixed gaze on her Mother, as she lowered herself into the chair.

"Mama what is it? You said happy tears!"

A look of confusion was on Alexandra's face.

"Yes baby! Steve is a good man! You know I'm never wrong about a person's character!"

"That's true Mama! God gave you a good gift."

"He's given you one too baby!" Mrs. Douglass softly spoke.

"What do you mean Mama?"

Mrs. Douglass smiled at Steve and nodded her head. Steve stood beside Alexandra, and quickly shifted his body toward her.

"What she means Alexandra, is that we had a little talk while you were in the kitchen, and your Mother gave me her permission to have your hand in marriage; that is, if you will have me!"

Alexandra was shocked by his words. She opened her mouth, but couldn't utter a single word, as she watched Steve lower his body to the floor. He positioned himself directly in front of her on one knee. Reaching into his back pocket, he removed a black velvet box; opening it to reveal the ring. Tears began to stream down Alexandra's face as she took in the beauty of the exquisite diamond ring.

"Alexandra, will you be my wife? I know we haven't been together long, but life is short! I love you, and I promise to be good to you! "

Alexandra remained silent and appeared to be frozen in the chair.

"Please marry me! You are the only woman I have ever wanted for my wife!"

He lovingly stared into her eyes as he waited for her to answer. She swallowed to clear the lump in her throat before she spoke.

"This really is sudden Steve!!"

"I know it is! But don't you love me, Alexandra? I have waited my whole life to see that look of genuine love in a beautiful woman's eyes; knowing it is just for me!"

Tears streamed down her face as she turned to look at her Mother.

"Mama, is this a dream?"

"No, it's real baby! Mrs. Douglass assured.

Steve placed his hand on Alexandra's chin, gently guiding her face back toward him, and found her eyes.

"Alexandra! Please say you'll be my bride! I know what I want! I promise to love you, and I will do everything I can to keep you happy! Please say you'll be my bride! I really love you, Alexandra!"

His sincere eyes pleaded for an answer, and his words melted into her heart.

"Yes! I will marry you, Steve!" she cried.

Steve removed the ring from the box and slipped it on her finger. She was amazed at the way the ring slid on with ease.

"Perfect fit! It's beautiful Steve!"

He tenderly kissed her on the lips, as the two of them embraced.

They quickly made their wedding plans and agreed on a simple ceremony at her Mother's bedside. They watched her deteriorate more each day. Alexandra prayed that she would live long enough to be present at their wedding. In one week's, time, the two of them arranged everything. They agreed to postpone the honeymoon until after Christmas, which was six weeks away. They wanted to settle everything with her Mother, and the new home the two of them would share. Each wanted a fresh start.

Their wedding day quickly arrived. The room was filled with fresh flowers, and their sweet

fragrance scented the air. Steve and his brother Pete stood beside the Minister who appeared to

tower over the two of them in his black suit and white collar. His Aunt Emily sat in the chair at Mrs. Douglass' bedside. The two of them were dressed in ivory gowns. They conversed as they waited for Pat and Alexandra. Pat entered the room first, wearing a yellow sleeveless gown and a white carnation in her hair. She carried a mixed bouquet of fresh flowers. Moonlight sonata played as she slowly walked in. She took her place beside the Minister, leaving enough space for Alexandra. Emily rose to her feet as the wedding march began to play. Pete made eyes at Pat as they waited for Alexandra to enter. She gracefully walked in. Her sleeveless, off the shoulder white gown was decorated with tiny beads, sequins, and lace. She purchased it off the rack from a small Bridal boutique in the area. She held her head high, as a beautiful tiara graced it. A dozen red roses rested upon her arm. Tears were in every eye. Steve stood tall, handsome, and proud, in his black Tuxedo. He suddenly became weak in the knees as he beheld the beauty of his bride.

Pete quickly intervened and supported him until he regained his composure.

"Who gives this woman to be married to this man?" the Minister asked.

"We do!" Mrs. Douglass' raspy voice sounded.

She tightly gripped the picture of her late husband, as it rested upon her chest. Alexandra and Steve exchanged vows, and rings before sharing their first kiss as Husband and Wife. They were congratulated by all. The newlyweds stood at Mrs. Douglass bedside.

"Welcome to the family son!" She whispered to Steve, offering a weak smile.

A beautiful glow spread across Alexandra's face. It had been quite a while since she had seen her Mother look so happy. She admired her beauty, as she lay on the bed in the gown the two of them selected online.

The white rose in her Mothers' long silver hair added just the right touch.

"Be happy baby!" Mrs. Douglass softly spoke.

"I am Mama!" Alexandra cried as she lovingly looked at her Mother.

She felt her husband's strong arms embrace her as the two of them remained at her Mother's bedside. Alexandra reached out and gently held her Mothers' hand. Mrs. Douglass smiled at the handsome couple, and took her final breath, as she inhaled the scent of the fresh flowers.

Chicken Wings

By Robin E. Thorpe

Ooh! I love Thanksgiving! The food, time with family, and the excitement in the air between Thanksgiving and New Year's Day; I love it!

The winter holidays have always been so special to me, but nothing could have prepared me for what I experienced that year. It's amazing how one day can change you, and the way you view the world forever.

My cousin Sharlisa has always teased me about being a "BRAT." She seems to think that because I'm the only child, I get everything I want. It's not my fault that there are seven of them in their house, and they never seem to have enough of anything to go around. I don't brag about what my parents have done for me, but she always tries to make me feel bad for being blessed. I don't have everything, and I'm not rich or privileged as some would say. I live a normal, everyday life like everyone else; at least that's what I thought until...

Let me tell you about my neighbor Miss Mabel. She stood about four foot ten and always had the nicest smile on her little round face. She reminded me of a baby doll. Every time she hugged me it was like being squeezed by big, fluffy pillows. She may have been small in stature, but she had the biggest heart of all the people I know; she would help anyone.

Every year on Christmas Eve you would see her going from house to house, wearing her fuzzy red hooded coat and pushing her wire basket with the wobbly wheel, making deliveries of her home baked cookies. You'd smell those cookies as soon as you opened the door, and I don't know how she did it, but every time I would open the can, those cookies would still be warm. I never understood how she did that, because Christmas Eve in Detroit was always cold, and our house was one of her last stops.

A few years ago, on one of those hot August nights about eleven o' clock, we started to smell something burning, and the house began filling up with smoke.

"Take that fan out of the window!" Mama yelled. "I don't know who's starting their barbecue at this time of night, but I sure don't want a house full of smoke! Hurry up and take it out boy!"

Daddy came running down the stairs. "That don't smell like no barbecue to me. I think something around here is on fire! "He shouted.

We all rushed out of the door and when we reached the sidewalk, we saw the top of Miss Mabel's house in flames. I can remember it like it was yesterday. Daddy running barefoot down the street with nothing on but his boxers. People swarmed from all over the neighborhood because if anyone was loved it was Miss Mabel. Daddy and Mr. Hanson our neighbor was the first to get to Miss Mabel's house. They ripped that door right off its hinges and rushed inside. A few minutes seemed like days as I waited clutching Mama's arm and looking for Daddy, Mr. Hanson, or Miss Mabel to come out of what had quickly become a wall of fire. I was scared for all of them. I remember how the distant sound of the sirens had become almost unbearable as they neared our street. My eyes must have become as big as two eight balls when I saw Daddy and Mr. Hanson come out carrying, Miss Mabel, and carefully laying her down on her front lawn. The paramedics rushed over and quickly placed an oxygen mask on her face. I don't know how long they fought that fire, but when it was over Miss Mabel's beautiful home had become a big, wet, pile of burnt wood. After the investigation, the fire chief said it was an electrical fire. They took Miss Mabel to the hospital. She had fallen and hurt her leg trying to get out of the house, so she inhaled too much smoke. I heard one of the firefighters say that if it wasn't for Daddy, and Mr.

Hanson getting her out when they did, she probably would not have made it.

A couple of days later Mama went to the hospital, but they told her that Miss Mabel had been discharged and that there was no further information, so we all thought that she must have gone to stay with relatives. A few months passed, and on the Eve of Thanksgiving, Mama was sitting at the kitchen table looking at the sale paper from one of the neighborhood markets. I smiled because I knew what was coming.

"Ronald! I need you to go to the store and get me some of these chicken wings!"

No matter how much she brought home from the supermarket, you can be certain that the day before, or on the day of the holiday, either Daddy or I would be asked to make that last minute run to the store. Daddy always teased her about it, and we would all laugh, but we understood that whatever it was that she wanted, we were going to hurry out of the house and get it, because we wanted whatever she was cooking. Mama sure can cook! Wait a minute! Did I just hear Mama say that she wanted some chicken wings?

"Mama. Did you forget that tomorrow is Thanksgiving? "

"You know son, they done cut your Daddies hours at work and we had to make some changes in
    the budget, so this year we're having chicken wings for dinner."

I can remember thinking that somehow Mama didn't understand that every year on Thanksgiving we have "THE FEAST".

"Mama, I don't mean no disrespect. But don't nobody want no chicken wings for Thanksgiving.

I want some turkey and dressing, ham, candied yams, homemade rolls, collard greens, macaroni, and cheese. You know "THE FEAST"!

Now Mama let me know that she understood how I felt, but she also let me know by the tone of her voice that it was time for me to make my way out of the door, or duck to avoid the "SMACK", that would soon be greeting the back of my head. I understood that this is the holiday when we're supposed to give thanks for all the blessings we have, but I couldn't see the good in having chicken wings for Thanksgiving. I fussed all the way to the market.

As soon as I was out of the market, I saw my boy Kenny, and he saw me too, so it was too late to hurry around the corner to avoid him. Best friends or not, sometimes you get in one of those old ugly sorts of moods when you don't want to see anybody you know, and I was certainly in one of those. We gave each other our usual brother to brother greeting while I tried to avoid eye contact, knowing that he would see right through my charade.

"Man, what are you looking so down about? I happen to know that tomorrow is one of your favorite days of the year, and I know that your moms is at home doing the same thing that mine is doing; hookin up tomorrow's dinner! Man, Mama 's cookin turkey, and dressin, ham, chittlins, greens, cornbread, mac and cheese, sweeeet potato pie, banana puddin, peach cobbler, and your favorite, her melt in your mouth chocolate cake."

Now if there was such a thing as someone putting salt in your wounds, Kenny dumped rock salt in mine.

"Man! Mama said all we're having is these stupid! stankin! chicken wings! She said something about the budget being tight this year. Don't nobody want to hear that at Thanksgiving! I want some turkey! And now I want some of your Mama's chocolate cake! How am I supposed to be thankful for some old chicken wings?"

"It could be a lot worse. Your moms makes the best fried chicken I've ever tasted! In fact, her chicken tastes better than my mama's turkey. I should be coming over to your house tomorrow!" he teased.

"If you do, you better be packing a big fat slice of your mama's Chocolate cake!" I responded as we both burst out in laughter, and then I heard the sweetest sound I've ever heard, Miss Mabel's voice.

"How's my boys doing?" she asked as she limped along dragging a huge cardboard box. The kind that you get when you buy a new refrigerator.

Kenny and I both ran over to hug her. As Kenny went into the store, I assisted Miss Mabel with the box. I don't think I even knew how much she meant to me until that moment.

"Where do you live now Miss Mabel?" I asked.

"Turn right here." She said walking into the alley.

Now I thought she was taking a shortcut to the senior apartments down the street, but nothing could have prepared me for what happened next.

"Did your Mother send you to the store?" she asked.

"Yeah, and can you believe she's only fixing these stupid chicken wings for Thanksgiving?"

"I'm sure she has a good reason son. Be thankful that you have your Mother's chicken. She's the best cook I know, so be very grateful, son. You need to be thankful that God put anything on your table! It's a lot of hungry people in this world son! Put that box right here next to this dumpster."

"You mean in the dumpster, don't you?" I questioned.

"Boy you better not throw my blanket away! That's what's gonna keep me warm tonight. It's real good protection from these winter winds!"

"Miss Mabel, you can't mean that you're going to spend the night out here?"

"Sure I am, son. This is my home now. I lost everything in that fire. This is not as bad as it looks, and God done give me good company, Mr. Joe, Annie, and Willie. We can all sleep real good tonight too, now that I have this box. We can put it in between these two dumpsters, and we'll be nice and warm." She said with the most satisfied smile on her face, as if she had gone shopping and found everything she wanted.

"Miss Mabel, I can't let you stay out here! My Mama would beat the fool out of me!"

"Well, you better not tell her unless you want a beatin!" she teased. Now hush all that fuss chile and help me git our Thanksgiving dinner! The others will be back soon."

When Miss Mabel started to walk over to the back door of the soul food restaurant, I thought that she was going to knock on the door for a carryout or something, but she walked right past it and stood in front of another dumpster that sat beside the door.

"Come on son and open this up for me so I can git dinner!"

The thought of Miss Mabel eating out of the garbage almost made me throw up, and the smell of the garbage didn't help either, especially when I opened the top.

"I can't let you eat out of the garbage, Miss Mabel!" I cried.

"Sure you can! Every night people go into that restaurant and order all kinds of food, and then they don't even eat half of what's on their plate. The rest is thrown out here; so, we don't let all of that good food go to waste. Sometimes we even git it while it's still warm. You see I haven't lost a pound. In fact, I think I may have even put on a few!"

She provided a bit of humor to what clearly become a serious moment for me. I was terrified at the thought of leaving her there eating out of the garbage. She turned and gave me her sweet twinkle eyed smile, and one of her pillow hugs.

"Now git on home boy, before your Mama starts to worry. It's beginning to git dark you know!"

"I can't leave you out here by yourself!" I reasoned.

"Here comes Mr. Joe right now, so you see I ain't alone, so git boy and Happy Thanksgivin to you, and your family."

The walk home seemed like the longest walk ever, and that bag of chicken wings felt as if it weighed fifty pounds. The next day at dinner, Daddy blessed the table as he did every day, and the smell of Mama's fried chicken could make even the strongest vegetarian beg for a bite, but I couldn't bring myself to put even one on my plate. I kept quiet, but the silence was eating me up.

"You feeling alright son?" Daddy asked because if it was one thing, he knew about me it was the fact that I never missed any meals.

"I hope you're not still upset about these chicken wings boy, we should be very thankful for whatever God blesses us with!" Mama added.

"I'm okay, and believe me, I've never been more grateful for anything than I am for this food!" I said.

Hanging my head in shame. The next thing I knew I was sobbing all over the dining room and telling them all about Miss Mabel. I asked if we could go and take some of the chicken wings to Miss Mabel and her friends. My parents agreed that it was the only right thing to do, so we wrapped everything in foil to keep it warm and joined them in the alley. Who would have ever thought we would be eating our Thanksgiving dinner in an alley sitting on milk crates?

They were all so glad to see us. Miss Mabel said that it was the happiest Thanksgiving she ever had, and in some ways, it was for me too. Other than the joy of giving, my favorite thing had to be watching Miss Mabel work those bones. That one day changed my whole world. I had a new appreciation for life, and all that the Lord blessed us with.

My parents offered to let Miss Mabel come and stay in our spare room, but she smiled and said she would let them know tomorrow. I was so excited to go back and get her that next day. I got in my clothes faster than I think I ever had before, but when we got to the alley the only ones we found were Mr. Joe, Annie, and Willie. They told us that Miss Mabel passed away about an hour after we left. They said she died with the biggest smile on her face. Although my heart was broken, and I thought my tears would never stop; I knew somehow that Miss Mabel was up in Heaven teaching everybody how to make her cookies and telling them all about Mama's chicken wings.

ALSO, BY THE AUTHORS

Ivy Lee's Rue **by Valerie D Wade**

This story follows Ivy Lee, a warm, compassionate, joyous woman from her childhood in rural North Carolina. The circumstances of her life were not ideal. When a life altering "condition" consumed her, she reached a crossroad. Family secrets and hushed decisions kept the one thing she loved out of reach. She held hope at the cliff of psychological madness, which consumed her life as she longed for peace, clarity, and joy.

Leaving Jacksonville **by Valerie D Wade**

Experience the captivating story of the great migration to Detroit through this thought-provoking novella. Gain insight into the challenges and triumphs of those who journeyed to this vibrant city seeking better opportunities. Explore themes of hope, resilience, and the pursuit of the American Dream.

☞ **Both books are available via** www.*Valeriewadeonline.com*

Coming Soon

The Other Hand **by Robin E. Thorpe**

Diane Harrington's night at the movie theater offers a brief encounter with a mysterious stranger Mr. Chase. As she welcomes his presence into her life, changes and challenges occur while juggling her career as a dance instructor, wife, and Mother.

The Other Hand creates moments of joy, suspense, laughter, and tears as the truth of the mysterious stranger unfolds. Diane's story may cause the reader to look closer to those they allow into their own lives.